THOMAS LOCKER

GRANDFATHER'S
CHRISTMAS
TREE

WRITTEN BY KEITH STRAND

Voyager Books • Harcourt, Inc.

SAN DIEGO   NEW YORK   LONDON

When I was a child, my family spent most of our holidays on my grandparents' ranch in northern Colorado. To a small boy from the city, it was heaven.

Of everything I remember, two things are most clear in my mind. First, is the single, tall blue spruce tree standing in front of my grandparents' home. The other is a small wooden nest cradling two carved geese and their five tiny goslings. Every year on Christmas Eve, I watched as my grandfather placed the little nest in the low branches of the blue spruce. One Christmas morning, when I was eight years old, I asked him why this was so. This is the story he told me.

My MOTHER AND FATHER came to Colorado in May of 1886. They had left their home in Illinois early that month, traveling westward on the railroad through Iowa and Nebraska, and finally into Colorado. Like so many others at that time, my parents longed to leave the crowded cities east of the Mississippi for the open country of the western frontier.

In Denver my parents bought horses, a wagon, and the supplies they would need to continue their journey. In mid-June they found this gentle valley, where low foothills push up against the towering Rocky Mountains. There was plenty of grass for grazing animals and trees good for firewood covered the hillsides. A clear-running stream drained the lowlands, near a small stand of blue spruce that would shelter a home from wind in the winter and the hot sun in July. They settled this piece of land and set to work making a new life together.

My father toiled all summer and into the fall, clearing land and building their first home. My mother cared for the animals, tended to the garden, and did whatever else needed doing.

One morning my mother told my father she had some wonderful news. "At Christmastide a baby will come," she told him. They felt grateful and very happy, but also just a little lonely. My parents realized for the first time how much they were truly on their own. The nearest town was half a day's wagon ride, and their closest neighbors lived four miles away.

By the third week of October, frost covered the land most mornings like a cold blanket. Every few days great flocks of geese flying south from Canada would swoop low over the ranch, searching for food and a place to rest. Winter would soon arrive, and my parents had done their best to be ready.

The house was complete enough to provide shelter, and my mother had been busy putting up vegetables and stocking the pantry. My father had hauled several cords of firewood down from the hills and had stacked the logs neatly outside the door.

But nothing could have prepared them for what was to come.

November and December of 1886 brought blizzards to these parts that sometimes howled for days on end. Snow piled into drifts six feet high, burying wagon trails, fences, and cattle. A rancher could go out for firewood or to check on his animals and become lost just fifty feet from his door. Even when the snow would let up for a while, the cold and wind continued. Though they loved each other deeply, my mother and father felt very, very alone.

Three weeks before Christmas, most of the logs my father had chopped and split had been burned in the woodstove. By then snow was higher than a horse's belly. There was no hope of leaving the ranch or of hauling more wood from the hills anytime soon. At that moment, my parents realized that they would have to start cutting down the blue spruce trees that sheltered the house if they hoped to survive the winter. Only the spruce could provide the firewood they so desperately needed.

Several days later, after my father had been chopping at one of the remaining trees for most of the morning, my mother went outside to call him in for lunch. While standing by the door, she noticed two geese huddled in the snow under the low boughs of the tallest blue spruce. This seemed peculiar to my mother, who remembered sadly how all of the geese had flown south soon after the first blizzards struck. She sorely missed the sight of the perfect chevrons they formed high in the sky.

As she slowly inched her way closer, she noticed that one of the great birds was injured. Its left wing bent at an odd angle, broken somehow. My mother gently called to my father to join her. Not being familiar with the ways of wild geese, my father startled the pair. The healthy bird hissed and pecked and flapped its wings.

My mother told my father how she had heard that geese, like people, pair for life. The big goose was protecting its injured mate, just as my folks would watch out for each other. My father agreed to leave the geese in peace and let nature take its course.

Late that night I was born.

Howling wind shook the walls and sleet splattered against the windows. To warm me, my mother held me to herself as my father covered us with a large, soft quilt. The light of the fire burning in the woodstove pierced the darkness. My father looked at the handsome woman lovingly cradling her babe.

His calm, deep voice cut through the roar of the squall. "Now we are a family," he said with pride.

The weather did not change much over the next two weeks. Every few days the storms came screaming out of the frozen sky, dropping great sheets of snow and ice, and chilling even the bravest hearts among the strong people who settled this land. Huge drifts of heavy snow nearly buried our door, and layers of frosty mist coated the windowpanes.

Christmas Eve arrived bitter cold, with high broken clouds. My father looked at our meager supply of logs and guessed we would burn them all within the next several weeks. He knew the time had come to cut down the towering spruce tree.

As my father was getting ready, my mother begged him not to take down the great tree just yet, knowing that if it was gone, the two geese sheltering under it would surely die. He said that without more firewood, we would not live to see the spring.

"We've endured much this winter," my mother said in a strong low voice. "You must believe that all will be well." The strength of her voice was soothing.

Finally my father agreed to leave the tree standing until Christmas Day had passed.

That night the moon cast its icy white light over the frozen valley. The wind rushed down from the mountains, rattling the windows as if in anger and blowing snow right through the tiniest gaps in the door frame. A new storm was coming to life.

My mother sang a lullaby as she gently rocked me to sleep. Her thoughts drifted to the geese. Since the day she had found them, my folks had helped keep them alive by piling handfuls of grain and leaving bowls of water under the spruce tree. These brave animals seemed almost part of our family. There had to be some way to save them.

As the night wore on the storm battered our home in all its fury. With a loud snap, the wind tore a giant branch from the spruce and sent it hurtling into the side of our house. The noise was fearsome but the cabin was strong. Finally my parents drifted to sleep huddled together hoping and praying for a miracle.

Christmas morning dawned bright and clear, with golden sunshine streaming through the windows and washing over the walls. My parents awoke to the sound of dripping water. They picked me up, pulled on their boots, and ran outside—my mother holding me, still asleep, in her arms.

Big slabs of slushy ice were breaking apart and sliding, with a crash, off the roof. The warm air was so still, not a whisper of wind could be heard. Brilliant sunlight blazed upon the snow.

Wrapping us tightly in his big embrace, my father said, "I know now that you are right, my dearest. All will be well under heaven."

All that following week, the sun bathed the valley in its mellow heat. By New Year's Day, much of the snow had melted, and my father was finally able to take the horses and haul more firewood down from the hills. The handsome spruce was left standing, all alone in front of the house. The geese sheltered under its branches, but as the weather warmed, they would venture out and about, honking and squawking to each other.

In late April my mother noticed the geese were building a nest by the stream. Every morning she took me to see it. Several weeks later, five baby chicks hatched.

That afternoon my mother asked my father to visit the nest with us. There she told him that another child would be born when the snow came that winter.

December of 1887 was mostly mild, with clear moonlit nights and sunny days. My folks stayed busy with their chores, all the while preparing for the new baby and caring for me. When he had a rare spare moment, my father would sit by the stove and carve figures out of wood. Shortly before Christmas, he carved a small wooden nest cradling two beautiful geese and their five babies.

Later that evening, while my father was cleaning wood shavings from the blade of his old knife, my mother whispered, "I think it is time."

My sister was born two days before my first birthday.

On Christmas Eve my father bundled me up and took me outside. We stood together at the base of the big blue spruce. As he held me close, my father stooped down and gently placed the small nest he had carved in the low boughs of the tree. Then he said with a soft smile, "Happy Christmas, little one."

So ends my grandfather's tale. More than fifty years have passed since he first told it to me. As a young man I moved to the ranch I had loved as a boy. I married and raised my family here.

Each Christmas Eve, for as long as I can recall, my family gathers in the shadow of the tree, which stands like a gentle giant beside our home. A breeze stirs the still night air. Twigs and needles sway as into the branches of the spruce I place the little wooden nest I first saw as a boy. For just a moment I hear my grandfather's strong voice carried on the wind. He tells me not to forget what he taught me.

www.HarcourtBooks.com

First Voyager Books edition 2002
*Voyager Book*s is a trademark of Harcourt, Inc., registered in
the United States of America and/or other jurisdictions.

The Library of Congress has cataloged the hardcover edition as follows:
Strand, Keith.
Grandfather's Christmas tree/by Keith Strand; illustrated by Thomas Locker.
p.   cm.
Summary: A grandfather tells how the family's Christmas
tradition of placing a carved wooden nest with a pair of geese
and their babies in the large spruce tree started years ago when
his parents first settled in Colorado.
[1. Frontier and pioneer life—Colorado—Fiction. 2. Geese—Fiction.
3. Christmas—Fiction. 4. Colorado—Fiction.]
I. Locker, Thomas, 1937– ill.   II. Title.
PZ7.S8965Gr 1999
[Fic]—dc21 98-13077
ISBN 0-15-201821-2
ISBN 0-15-216374-3 pb

HGFEDCBA

To my wife, Anne,
my son, Michael,
my daughter, Sarah,
and to my mother, Gloria
—K. S.

To Kaulini, from Grandpa
—T. L.

The illustrations in this book were done in oils on canvas.
The display type was set in Birch and Madrone.
The text type was set in Bembo.
Color separations by Bright Arts Ltd., Hong Kong
Manufactured by South China Printing Company, Ltd., China
Production supervision by Sandra Grebenar and Wendi Taylor
Designed by Michael Farmer

This Book Belongs To

_____

It's the Great Pumpkin,
Charlie Brown

SIMON SPOTLIGHT
An imprint of Simon & Schuster Children's Publishing Division
1230 Avenue of the Americas, New York, New York 10020
This Simon Spotlight edition July 2018
© 2018 Peanuts Worldwide LLC
For information about special discounts for bulk purchases, please contact Simon & Schuster
Special Sales at 1-866-506-1949 or business@simonandschuster.com.
Manufactured in China 0518 SCP
2 4 6 8 10 9 7 5 3 1
ISBN 978-1-5344-1394-8
ISBN 978-1-5344-1395-5 (eBook)

PEANUTS®

It's the Great Pumpkin,
Charlie Brown

By Charles M. Schulz
Based on the animated special, the text was adapted by Maggie Testa
Illustrated by Vicki Scott

Simon Spotlight
New York London Toronto Sydney New Delhi

It was a special time of year. The air felt brisk and cool. The colorful leaves fell from the trees. The pumpkins were ready to be picked. It was fall, and for Linus, Lucy, Snoopy, and Charlie Brown, that meant Halloween was almost here.

It also meant football. One afternoon, Lucy approached Charlie Brown. "I'll hold the ball, and you come running and kick it," she said sweetly.

But Charlie Brown shook his head. He knew what Lucy was up to. "You just want me to come running up to kick that ball so you can pull it away and see me land flat on my back."

"This time you can trust me," said Lucy. She held out a piece of paper. "See? Here's a signed document testifying that I promise not to pull it away."

He felt excited. This year he was really going to kick that football. Charlie Brown got a running start, but as usual, Lucy pulled the ball away as he got close. "Aaugh!" cried Charlie Brown as he flew into the air.

"Peculiar thing about this document," said Lucy, "it was never notarized."

Meanwhile, Linus was busy with his own fall tradition. He was writing his annual letter to the Great Pumpkin.

Dear Great Pumpkin, Linus began. *I am looking forward to your arrival on Halloween night. I hope you will bring me lots of presents.*

Charlie Brown was curious. "Who are you writing to?" he asked.

Linus smiled, and then he explained, "This is the time of year to write to the Great Pumpkin. On Halloween night, the Great Pumpkin rises out of his pumpkin patch and flies through the air with a bag of toys for all the children."

Charlie Brown just shook his head as he walked away. Even Snoopy laughed as he walked by.

Linus kept on writing. Soon his sister, Lucy, came by.

"Not again," Lucy complained over his shoulder. "Writing a letter to a pumpkin? You make me the laughingstock of the neighborhood."

But Linus still wrote, *Everyone tells me you are a fake, but I believe in you.*

A little while later, Sally walked over. She wanted to know what Linus was doing.

Linus told her all about the Great Pumpkin. "Would you like to sit with me in the pumpkin patch on Halloween night and wait for the Great Pumpkin?"

"I'd love to, Linus!" said Sally.

Finally, Linus was finished writing his letter.

"And how do you think you're going to mail that letter?" Lucy asked. "You can't possibly reach the mailbox, and I'm not going to help you."

But Linus had an idea. He used his blanket like a lasso to open the mailbox. Then he tossed the letter in. Nothing could stop him from sending his letter to the Great Pumpkin!

As Linus went proudly back inside, Charlie Brown came running up to Lucy.

"I got an invitation to a Halloween party!" Charlie Brown told her. He did a happy dance. "It's the first time I've ever been invited to a party."

Lucy frowned. "If you got an invitation, it was a mistake. There were two lists. One to invite and one not to invite. You must have been put on the wrong list."

But Charlie Brown didn't care what Lucy said. He had his invitation, and he was going to that Halloween party!

Soon it was Halloween night. The kids all changed into their costumes for trick-or-treating. Lucy was a witch. Sally was a ghost. She was afraid of her own costume! Charlie Brown was also a ghost, but he had a little trouble with the scissors. Pigpen was a ghost . . . a very dirty one!

Even Snoopy had dressed up. He was a World War I Flying Ace.

"Now I've heard everything!" exclaimed Lucy.

As Snoopy marched in a different direction, the little group hurried off to start trick-or-treating. They soon ran into Linus in the pumpkin patch.

"Have you come to sing pumpkin carols?" he asked them.

"You're going to miss all the fun, just like last year," Lucy told him.

But Linus didn't care. He knew the Great Pumpkin was on his way to this pumpkin patch.

"You really think he'll come?" Sally asked. As everyone left to go trick-or-treating, she was torn. Should she go with them or stay with Linus?

Sally decided to stay!

"I'm glad," said Linus. "You'll see the Great Pumpkin with your own eyes. Each year, the Great Pumpkin rises out of the pumpkin patch that he thinks is the most sincere. He's got to pick this one! I don't see how a pumpkin patch could be more sincere than this one."

Meanwhile, the other kids had arrived at their first house of the night. "Tricks or treats!" they cried. One by one, candy was thrown into their bags.

"Can I have an extra piece of candy for my brother?" Lucy asked. "He couldn't come with us 'cause he's sitting in a pumpkin patch waiting for the Great Pumpkin."

The kids compared what they got.

"I got five pieces of candy," said Lucy.

"I got a chocolate bar," said Violet.

"I got a quarter," said Schroeder.

"I got a rock," said Charlie Brown.

Soon everyone's bags were filled with candy, except Charlie Brown's. His bag was filled with rocks. But he didn't let that get him down. It was time to go to the Halloween party!

On the way, Violet wondered where Snoopy, the World War I Flying Ace, had gone.

"He's probably getting ready to take off on the next dawn patrol," answered Charlie Brown.

Soon the group passed by the pumpkin patch.

"Has the Great Pumpkin been by?" taunted Violet.

"You think you're so smart," Sally called as the laughing group continued along. "He'll be here. You can bet on that!"

Sally turned to Linus. "All right, where is he?"

"He'll be here," Linus assured her.

"I hope so," said Sally. "Just think of all the fun we're missing!"

Across town, the Halloween party was in full swing. There were games, and music, and pumpkins to decorate.

Violet, Patty, and Lucy wanted to draw the perfect face on their pumpkin, but how would they know what to draw on it?

"You'll have to model for us," Violet told Charlie Brown.

"You'll be the perfect model," agreed Patty.

Charlie Brown felt honored. He sat down on a stool. Violet turned him around. That's when he realized they wanted to use the back of his head as a model for the pumpkin!

Next it was time to bob for apples. Lucy went first. "This is the way to do it." She stuck her head in the barrel and came up with an apple . . . and Snoopy!

"Blech!" she cried. "My lips touched dog lips!"

Snoopy danced along while Schroeder played the piano. Then he figured it was time to continue on his journey as the World War I Flying Ace. He sniffed his way to the pumpkin patch.

Sally was just about fed up. Where was the Great Pumpkin?

Linus tried to reassure her. "Just think, Sally, when the Great Pumpkin rises out of the pumpkin patch, we'll be here to see him!"

All of a sudden, Linus heard a noise. "What's that?" he asked.

He watched as a dark figure appeared in the pumpkin patch. "There he is! It's the Great Pumpkin!" Linus shouted. He was so excited that he fainted!

When Linus awoke, Sally was waiting for him.

"What happened?" Linus asked. "What did the Great Pumpkin leave us? Did he leave us any toys?"

Sally couldn't contain her frustration any longer. "I was robbed!" she shouted. "I spent the whole night waiting for the Great Pumpkin when I could have been out for tricks or treats! Halloween is over and I missed it!" She pointed at Linus. "You kept me up all night waiting for the Great Pumpkin, and all that came was a beagle!"

As Sally left, Linus called after her. "It won't be long now," he said. "If the Great Pumpkin comes, I'll still put in a good word for you."

Linus gasped. He said "if." Was he starting to doubt the Great Pumpkin too?

The hours ticked by. After a while, Linus fell asleep. He was shivering under his blanket when Lucy came out to get him in the very early hours of the morning and tuck him into bed.

Later that day, Charlie Brown and Linus met up.

"Well, another Halloween has come and gone," said Charlie Brown. "I don't understand it. I went trick-or-treating and all I got was a bagful of rocks."

Charlie Brown looked at his friend. "I suppose you spent all night in the pumpkin patch and the Great Pumpkin never showed up."

"Nope," said Linus.

"Don't take it too hard, Linus," Charlie Brown said. "I've done a lot of stupid things in my life too."

Linus furrowed his brows. "Stupid? What do you mean, stupid? Just wait till next year, Charlie Brown. You'll see. Next year I'll find a pumpkin patch that is really sincere, and I'll sit in that pumpkin patch until the Great Pumpkin appears!"